Elephant was very proud that he was the largest, strongest, and best animal. He boasted about it all the time.

AF594616

One day, the Rain Spirit heard about Elephant's boasting and decided to visit him.

"How can you possibly be larger, stronger, and better than me?" he quizzed Elephant.

Elephant replied, “Look at my long, pointed tusks. Look how the Earth shakes when I stamp my feet. No one argues with me. Of course I am the largest and the strongest.”

The Rain Spirit shook his head. “I fill the lakes and rivers so everyone can drink. Because of me, the crops can grow. That is far more important than your tusks and your stamping.”

Elephant was annoyed, so he waved his trunk and stamped his feet. “I find my own food and drink. I take care of myself. I don’t need you!” he trumpeted.

The Rain Spirit became angry. Dark clouds rolled across the sky and thunder rumbled.

"Well," thundered the Rain Spirit, "in that case, good luck! I will leave you to care for yourself," and with that the Rain Spirit vanished.

Elephant smiled. “See,” he announced, “I am the best. Even the Rain Spirit doesn’t frighten me.” Elephant was even more proud of himself. He kept on telling all of the other animals how he was the strongest and the best.

But when the rainy season came, no rain fell. The lakes and rivers dried up, and the crops died. The other animals came to see Elephant and begged him to make the rain fall. Elephant didn't know what to do. He shuffled his big strong feet, and clouds of dust blew up into the air. He dug with his long strong tusks, but found nothing. No underground river or stream.

“Tell Crow to make it rain,” he huffed. So Crow flew up to the sky and collected a few clouds together, and soon there was a short shower of rain.

The animals were very thirsty, and soon drank all of the rain that had fallen. Elephant had taken the biggest puddle for himself and he wouldn't let any of the other animals drink from it. He told Tortoise to guard it while he went to find something to eat.

The other animals approached the puddle.

"Go away!" shouted Tortoise. "This puddle is for Elephant only, no one else."

"But we are so thirsty," said Springbok and Zebra. They begged Tortoise to let them have just a sip from the puddle.

"No!" said Tortoise shaking his head. "Not a single drop."

But then Lion arrived. “You can’t drink here,” said Tortoise quickly. Lion looked down at Tortoise.

“Why not?” he said lazily.

“Because this puddle belongs to Elephant,” replied Tortoise importantly.

“Humph!” said Lion. He flicked his paw, and Tortoise went tumbling head over shell across the ground.

Tortoise didn't stop until he was a long way away from the puddle. Lion bent and lapped from the puddle, and all of the other animals rushed to get a drink, too.

Later, when Elephant returned, he was very angry and blamed Tortoise.

“I tried to stop them,” said Tortoise, “but Lion was too big and strong for me.”

Elephant was so angry that he picked Tortoise up with his trunk, popped him into his mouth, and gulped him down whole.

Inside Elephant, Tortoise stamped and stomped and butted the walls of Elephant's tummy.

"Stop!" shouted Elephant, but Tortoise kept on. All the stomping and stamping made Elephant feel very unwell. "Please stop," he pleaded, lying down to try and feel better.

Elephant was making so much noise that he attracted the notice of the Rain Spirit.

"Help! Please help me", begged Elephant.

"Me? Help you, the largest and strongest being in the land?" replied the Rain Spirit.

"Yes, please help me. I admit you are better and stronger than me. Please help," whimpered Elephant.

The Rain Spirit started to chuckle. As he chuckled, clouds gathered in the sky. Then rain burst out of the clouds and poured down over the land. Just then Tortoise gave such an enormous thump that Elephant sneezed and croaked, and Tortoise shot out of Elephant's mouth and tumbled out onto the ground.

"I will not help you again. You are not better than the other animals, nor are you kind," the Rain Spirit told Elephant.

Elephant looked down at the ground and apologized. "You are right," he said humbly. He ambled off, with his head down, and never again claimed that he was the largest, the strongest, or the best.